AUTUMN MOONBEAM

DANCE MAGIC!

EMMA FINLAYSON-PALMER & HEIDI CANNON

uclanpublishing

AUTUMN MOONBEAM

KNOTWEED MOONBEAM

STORM

MORDECAI AND
TOADFLAX MOONBEAM

GHOSTLY GRAN

SILVER MOONBEAM
(AKA MUM)

TREVOR

ZEPHYR MOONBEAM

EDITH 'BATTY' BATTINGTON

SEVERINA BLOODWORTH

LEIF KERRSE

MR SNAILCRUNCHER

MISS SPINNINGWEB

ONYX DARKSTONE

COSMIC-CREEPER

VERITY CHARM

SKYE
CLOUDSKIPPER

RAINBOW
CLOUDSKIPPER

MOONBEAMS AND CARTWHEELS

AUTUMN MOONBEAM leapt from her bed and cartwheeled across her room, leaving a trail of yellow swirls of light behind her.

"Do you have to do that in here?" Zephyr, Autumn's twin, said from the bottom bunk bed. She was busy playing chess with Ghostly Gran. It was a bit tricky as Zephyr had to move the pieces for her but she loved board games.

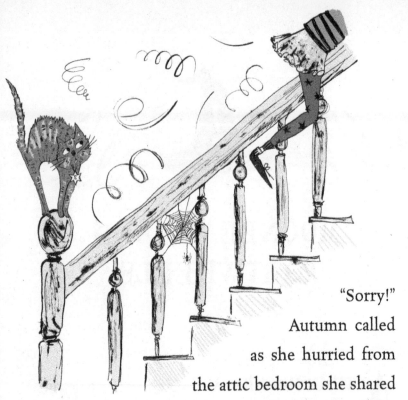

"Sorry!" Autumn called as she hurried from the attic bedroom she shared with her sister. She slid down the bannister, startling Storm as she did so. His scruffy grey fur stood on end and he miaowed once before trotting after her.

It was Saturday morning and she couldn't wait for her favourite dance show on the spell-a-vision to start. Autumn absolutely loved gymnastics and dance.

"A most wonderful gymnast," Miss Spinningweb had said. She would know – her PE teacher was in the gym team for the Aaarghlympics.

The kitchen table was already in chaos as Autumn's two older brothers, Mordecai and Toadflax, were making their way through fried snail's eggs on earwig toast for breakfast. There was no sign of her younger brother, Knotweed, who they always called Weed for short. Autumn knew that she had an amazing family but they were always so loud, so noisy, so messy and, most of all, they always got in her way when she was practising her dance magic.

Autumn poured herself some Beetlebix, stretching her leg up on the kitchen counter as she ate.

"No dancing in the kitchen. You're eight now, pumpkin, you know not to do it!" Mum breezed in from the garden, carrying Autumn's grubby little brother under one arm and a baby dragon under the

other. She plonked Weed down in his highchair at the table while Trevor – the dragon – squirmed free of her grasp and scampered off before he could be confined too.

Autumn sighed and reluctantly lowered her leg. "It's not dancing; I'm stretching."

"OK, no stretching in the kitchen then!"

Autumn loved to dance at home but someone or something always seemed to stop her. She wished she could go to a proper dance club instead, although her tummy filled with moths each time she thought about dancing in front of others.

She swallowed the last of her Beetlebix, plopped her bowl in the washing cauldron and skipped out of the kitchen before anyone else did. As Autumn skipped, little wisps of green glitter fluttered around her ankles.

Autumn clicked the spell-a-vision handset and images popped out of a little box in the corner of the living room. An advert for cat food was on and Storm miaowed at the kitten floating above them.

Autumn hopped on the spot with excitement as the dance judges appeared. One arrived in a big puff of sparkly gold smoke, followed by another who emerged from behind a cloud of bats.

She *Oooh'd* at their grand entrance and clapped along with the studio audience.

The first contestants were up and leaving a trail of fire behind them across the stage. Autumn decided it was best if she didn't try to copy their moves in the living room – her mum would never forgive her if she accidentally burned down the house!

Next a rainbow of butterflies circled the dancer expertly spinning and leaping across the stage. Autumn lifted her leg, trying to copy the witch's dancing.

She leapt into a star shape, arms outstretched, and a couple of butterflies fluttered around her hands.

"Flaming frogs' bottoms! I'm doing it."

Autumn's dance magic happiness was cut short as Weed came running in and bumped into her. The butterflies that had been fluttering around her hands turned a gargoyle-grey, made a hiss and a pop and were gone.

"Dance! Dance!" Knotweed called.

"Oh, Weed. You burst my butterflies!"

But she couldn't stay cross, and so they danced together. They leapt around the living room making up silly moves, giggling, and totally out of time with the dancers on the spell-a-vision. Their dance moves created noises like they were squelching through mud and made brown foamy clouds appear. Autumn laughed as Weed clapped and chased the clouds.

It was fun but Autumn really wished she could have the chance to dance uninterrupted, at a proper dance club.

WHAT I'D ALWAYS WISHED FOR!

IT WAS MONDAY, and Autumn was excited to talk to her friends about the dances she'd watched on the spell-a-vision. Autumn zoomed and looped on her broomstick, thinking about all the dancers she'd seen. Zephyr flew alongside with her headphones on, listening to a book about chess.

"Hey, bestie!" It was Edith Battington, although no one ever called her Edith. Everyone called her Batty instead because she had a little bat-shaped birthmark on her cheek.

She and Autumn had known each other since starting school and had been best friends ever since. They both loved gymnastics and dance, and Batty was always coming over so they could practise together in Autumn's garden.

"I even created butterflies when I swirled," Autumn told her.

Batty's eyes were as round as cauldrons. "Did you see the dance troupe that created fire with their moves? They were spell-tacular!" she said dreamily.

They parked their broom-sticks in the shed outside Pointy Hat Primary as their other friend, Leif Kerrse, pulled up.

The friends headed to their classroom for Potions – their first lesson of the day.

"Hi Skye!" Leif waved. A witch from the year below grinned back at him before doing a handstand into a bridge on the grass outside school. An arch of pink and purple twinkled above her and her friends clapped and cheered.

"Wow! She's amazing," Autumn said.

"She's in my team at Sparkledale Dance Academy," Leif said.

"Wish I could go there too!" Autumn skipped on the spot.

"I nearly forgot!" Leif plonked his rucksack on the desk in the Potions class and pulled out some leaflets. "Here, one for you and for you too, Batty. I'm guessing you won't want one, Zeph," Leif laughed.

"Not if it's dance-related," Zephyr smiled and organised her pens and wand neatly on her desk. Autumn was sure she was setting up her equipment like she would a strategic board game.

A witch animation backflipped over shimmering silver and turquoise letters on the piece of paper. Underneath it said:

Sparkledale Dance Academy

Limited places available in
Black Cats, our competitive dance team.
Try outs on Saturday at 1pm!

A black cat drawing stretched and curled at the

bottom of the leaflet then rubbed its head against the lettering.

Before Autumn had even finished reading, the leaflet was snatched from her grasp. "You're not going to try out are you, Moon-flop?" came a sneering voice. Severina was Autumn's neighbour and a general annoying know-it-all.

Autumn tried to get the leaflet back but Severina held it out of her reach. She knew Severina was really good at gym and dance, she'd seen her prancing about her back garden making all sorts of dance magic. Severina Bloodworth's parents were always getting her new things; she even had a big stage where she could dance as much as she wanted. She didn't have brothers getting in her way every five minutes.

Mr Snailcruncher cleared his throat and raised an eyebrow until they sat back at their desks. "OK, class, today we'll be making a potion to turn ourselves into an animal."

Cauldrons bubbled and steam of all different colours swirled as the potions heated up on each desk.

Mr Snailcruncher offered the choice of an extra ingredient to finish the potion. Autumn chose a hair and wondered what sort of animal it belonged to. She dropped it into the potion and it fizzed and smelt of mouldy cabbages. "Yuk!" She held her nose as she took a sip. It tasted of liquorice and frogs.

Autumn wrinkled her nose, then fur sprouted over her whole body . . . and a curly pink tail. Her skin felt like she was being stung with nettles.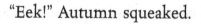

"Eek!" Autumn squeaked.

Zephyr had turned into an owl next to her. *Typical Zeph*, Autumn thought, *a really smart creature is perfect for her. I hope she doesn't eat me.*

"Well done," Mr Snailcruncher beamed, looking round at the classroom full of animals. "It'll wear off in about five minutes."

Autumn was relieved. She didn't fancy staying as a little mouse for much longer. Especially with Severina nearby eyeing her hungrily and flicking her new cat tail.

✳ ✳ ✳

After lunch they were in PE, Autumn's favourite lesson, with Miss Spinningweb. Autumn was glad to be back to her bouncy, witchy self after potion class.

Miss Spinningweb put the class into two teams to play dodgeball.

"Are you going to try out for Black Cats?" Batty whispered between dodges.

"You definitely should," Zephyr said. "You're statistically a very good dancer. And imagine not having brothers under your feet when you danced!"

"Joining a dance academy is what I've always wished for." Autumn twirled and a swirl of gold glittered around her.

"I'm going to try out," Severina butted in, flicking her long green hair over her shoulder. Batty rolled her eyes.

Severina would, Autumn thought. *She's really good too!* It took the sparkle from her thoughts and nervous moths fluttered in her tummy.

"Shall I come to yours after school tomorrow and we can practise together?" said Batty.

"Can I come too?" Leif asked. "I can show you some moves. I'd love it if you two were chosen for the team. There's only a few places though, so I'll keep my wands crossed for luck."

"That would be brilliant!" Autumn said cheerily, but deep down she was already worried that she wouldn't be chosen. Especially if Severina tried out too. A gloomy cloud of doubt settled over her.

WORRIES AND
WEBOLINES

"ANSWER THE DOOR!" Autumn's house filled
with shrieking from the enchanted doorbell.

"Hi, Autumn," Batty and Leif said in unison as
they stood on the doorstep.

Autumn was really excited to be dancing with
her friends. *I bet Leif knows lots of great stuff we could
do*, she thought.

"Great top," Batty said.

"Thanks." Autumn twirled to show off the sparkles that spelt out the words on her t-shirt: *Glitter, Bows and Pointed Toes.*

Autumn and her friends ducked as her older brothers rushed past, casting stink bomb spells at one another.

"Not in the house!" Mum shouted, freezing the stink bombs mid-air. "It took me weeks to get the smell out of the living room last time."

"Sorry, Mum," her brothers said, and pushed past Autumn and her friends as they ran through the front door.

"Your house is fun," Leif said. "There's only me and my little sister at mine."

"You probably wouldn't

think it was fun if you had to put up with my brothers every day," said Autumn. "There's never any peace."

Autumn stepped backwards as Ghostly Gran floated through the wall into the kitchen. It didn't hurt when you accidentally walked through her, but it was like getting dunked headfirst into a bath of ice cubes.

"Hi, Gran." Autumn waved. Gran waved back as she drifted by.

"Cool," said Leif. "Did you know that ghosts are terrible at lying?"

"Really?" Autumn asked.

"Yep, it's because . . . you can see right through them!" Leif doubled over, laughing at his own joke.

Batty rolled her eyes. "Leif, never mind ghosts being terrible at lying . . . your *jokes* are terrible!"

"Come on, let's head out to the garden." Autumn led her friends through the house towards the back door. They had to dodge Weed, who was playing a game of snakes and ladders on the kitchen floor. A snake had already eaten one of the ladders and Trevor the baby dragon was chewing on another one.

"Careful with dramatic dance moves, pumpkins. I don't want to have to use the bone fixing spell!" Mum warned.

"We'll be fine, Mum!" Autumn called.

"Hi, Zeph!" Batty and Leif waved at Zephyr, who was sitting cross-legged reading an Arithmancy book under the willow tree. She smiled and waved back before turning to the next page of her book.

"I've brought my collection of 'Witches of Dance and Gym' cards if anyone has any they want to swap?" Batty waved a big wedge of cards in her hand.

"You must have the biggest collection of cards I've ever seen!" Leif looked impressed.

"That is a massive collection, Batty," Zephyr said, numbers floating in the air above her head from the magic book.

"Thanks, I've been collecting them for ages." Batty beamed with pride at her cards.

"You should see my collection of board games." Zephyr grinned.

"OK, we're not here to talk about board

games, we're here to dance!" Autumn twirled on the spot and a spiral of glitter fluttered around her.

"Is that where Severina lives?" Leif whispered, pointing over the fence at the large building next door.

"Yep," Autumn said and fussed over Storm who was weaving around her legs.

"Shame we don't live next door to you instead," Leif smiled.

"I would definitely prefer you guys as neighbours." Autumn looked across to the fence that separated her garden from Severina's, just next to the big weeping willow. Storm had curled up in his favourite spot under the branches, next to Zephyr.

"Let's get to work." Batty was already jogging on the spot. "How about you magic up that weboline like you did the other day?"

Autumn flourished her wand and chanted, "Abracadoodle, bibbity bing, give me a thing with a spingitty spring!"

The sickly-sweet smell of toffee apples filled the

air and blue sparkles flew out from her wand. Long, thin glistening strands wove around and around until they formed a giant spider's web trampoline.

All three witches stretched and warmed up and were soon ready to train.

Zephyr looked up from her book and said, "If a witch dances ten routines and does five really well, the probability of getting a place is five out of ten and the odds of success would be fifty-fifty." Numbers and mathematical symbols floated around in a sparkly cloud as Zephyr spoke.

Autumn thought how much Zephyr sounded like their maths teacher, but that was no surprise as maths was Zephyr's favourite lesson.

"That sounds like a whole other language," said Batty, frowning in concentration.

"You're not exactly reassuring me, Zeph!" Autumn's tummy flipped and flopped and felt like she'd been splatted by a dodge ball.

Leif went through some simple moves like forward and backward rolls, cartwheels and handstands.

"I'll show you a dance routine," Leif said. He leapt around the garden swishing his arms about like a fluttering butterfly. As he moved, there was a tinging sound like wind chimes blowing in the breeze and birds singing. Leif glowed with a shimmering green.

"Wow, that was really magic, Leif!" said Autumn.

"Dancing dragons! You're brilliant!" Batty whooped.

"It's quite good, I suppose, but I can do better." Severina was leaning on the fence watching them. "Watch this!"

"She's so rude," Batty muttered. But the friends moved closer to the fence so they could see better.

Severina launched herself into an impressive series of cartwheels, then stopped halfway through one and walked in a big circle on her hands. Her legs pointed like wands criss-crossing in the air. There were swirls of pink and purple weaving together around her.

Autumn hated to admit it but Severina was amazing. She was just about to say as much when an almighty yowl interrupted her.

MIIAAOOWFTTTTZZZ!

Storm leapt up as Ghostly Gran floated right through him. He hissed angrily and startled Severina, who stumbled backwards as the ice-cold ghost drifted through the fence.

"Arrrgh! Freezing!" Severina shouted. The swirls of pink and purple turned grey and smelt like rotten frog's breath. Autumn, Batty, Leif and Zephyr held their noses and batted the air to try and swish the pongy smell away.

"Sorry, Severina!" Autumn said.

"Save it Moon-flop! Your family get everywhere… and they're so annoying!" And with that, Severina turned her back and stomped off to her house, slamming the door behind her.

As much as Autumn wanted to disagree, her family *did* get everywhere. She couldn't dance anywhere at home without falling over someone. Autumn was even more determined than before to be successful at the try outs.

I *need to be part of the Sparkledale Dance Academy!* she thought.

SPARKLEDALE
DANCE ACADEMY

AUTUMN GAZED in wonder at a sign with a witch animation backflipping over shimmering silver and turquoise letters. Her heart beat hard and fast, like it was pounding out an entire dance routine. Today was the day she had been waiting for – try outs for the competitive team at the Sparkledale Dance Academy.

"Good luck, pumpkin!" said Mum, giving Autumn a squeeze.

Autumn felt her cheeks flush. "Thanks," she said, looking around to make sure no one else had heard her mum use her special nickname.

"Ooh, I'm sooo proud of you, trying out for Black Cats!"

"Muuum!" Autumn groaned.

"OK, OK, I'll go. Weed, say bye to your sister." Autumn's little brother waved a grubby hand as he squirmed in Mum's arms.

"Good luck," Zephyr said, a board game tucked under one arm. "Remember, you've got a strong chance to get a place today."

"Thanks, Zeph. Have fun with your games today."

Zephyr grinned and rubbed her hands together.

"I'm going to take great delight in defeating all the other witches at the board game cafe. *Muahahaha!*"

If she wasn't so nervous, Autumn would have laughed at Zephyr's evil villain impression. Autumn took a deep breath as her mum, Zephyr and youngest brother left. The club foyer was full of other witches, with a sea of ponytails in every hair colour possible. She was relieved to see there were a lot of other anxious-looking faces that mirrored her own. But then she remembered there were only four spaces and there were a lot more than four witches trying out. She gulped.

"Hey, bestie!" called Batty.

Autumn skipped on the spot, little wisps of green glitter fluttering around her ankles as she hugged Batty. She was relieved to have her friend at her side.

"I'm so excited that we get to try out for Black Cats together," Autumn said.

"Me too! Have you seen all of these?" Batty pulled

Autumn by the arm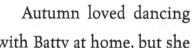
and pointed to a wall
covered in photos
of different teams
holding trophies and
wearing medals. "One
day that might be us!"

Autumn loved dancing
with Batty at home, but she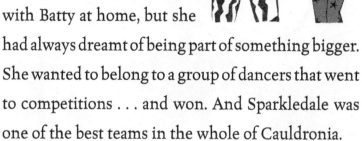
had always dreamt of being part of something bigger.
She wanted to belong to a group of dancers that went
to competitions . . . and won. And Sparkledale was
one of the best teams in the whole of Cauldronia.

"Wow, this is amazing!" Autumn imagined
herself posing for a photo with a team. Even the
word *team* made her breathless with excitement.
*And maybe I wouldn't feel shy or embarrassed if I was
with a team,* she thought.

Just at that moment, Verity Charm, the head

coach and owner, emerged from inside the gym with a dancer on either side of her. All three had matching midnight grey tops; purple sequins spelt out the word *Coach*, and in turquoise sequins across the back was the club name: *Sparkledale*.

Verity had a mass of curly dark hair pulled into a high ponytail that bounced as she moved and was held in place by a bow covered in little black cats. She was tall and Autumn could see that she had well-defined muscles from years of training.

"Good morning, everyone. Welcome to Sparkledale Dance Academy. I'm thrilled to see so many trying out for the competitive troupe." A black cat wound around her legs as she spoke. "Looks like Cosmic-Creeper wants to say hello."

Verity picked up the cat and he curled himself tightly in her arms. His bright yellow eyes scanned the dancers and he miaowed loudly.

"Cosmic-Creeper is our club mascot; the day I opened the club he turned up and decided to adopt us! He's been here ever since. Cosmic-Creeper is a special coach who will keep an eye out for you while you train," said Verity, smiling. "He's also good at sniffing out magic," she added, and tapped her nose.

Autumn shuffled on the spot, itching to give the cat a fuss; she loved cats.

"During training we will be using dance magic, but we'll keep it basic today. Magic must be handled with respect and care to keep us safe." Verity's smile faded. "And you must never use magic against another witch in this club."

There was a ripple of murmurs.

"I hope everyone is paying attention, as this is very important if you want to be a competitive dancer here," Verity continued; a serious expression on her face. "This is all about being the best athlete you can be, not about using enchantments to enhance performance or play tricks on others."

Cosmic-Creeper hopped down and wove his way towards the gym until he disappeared inside.

"This is Onyx and Rainbow." Verity gestured towards the two witches either side of her. Rainbow only came up to Verity's shoulder and her long, wavy turquoise hair reminded Autumn of a mermaid. Onyx used a wheelchair and had black straight hair and looked as if she lifted dragons for a living. They couldn't have been more different. "They help with coaching at the Black Cats training sessions."

Rainbow waved excitedly, while Onyx smiled and nodded in greeting.

Verity grinned so widely you could see almost every one of her dazzling white teeth. A performer's smile! "Now, change into your indoor trainers or pumps then come through to the gym and we'll get started."

She bounded through some doors and out of sight. Autumn swallowed hard as she followed the crowd. The gym was huge, with a high ceiling and one whole wall made up entirely of mirrors. Another wall had shelves full of trophies and banners that read *Grand Champion*.

There was a large pile of mats at one end of the gym and a long inflatable runway called a tumble track.

Autumn and Batty joined a queue for their try out number. Rainbow and Onyx were sitting at a table.

"Here you go." Rainbow handed Autumn a number twenty-two.

Onyx chanted: "Number stick, number quick!" A small puff of blue smoke spiralled, and the number placed itself on to Autumn's t-shirt by magic.

Autumn's arms prickled with goosebumps; it was cold in the gym. She took a deep breath, rubbed her arms and went across to the mats.

Verity walked alongside Autumn. "It's a little cool in here now but once you're training, you'll soon warm up."

Autumn smiled shyly. "This floor feels great," she said, and she stood on tiptoes and bounced gently.

"It'll help you get the bounce to spring into moves," said Verity kindly, moving away.

Autumn swallowed nervously; her throat dry. She stared at Batty in sudden panic, all her confidence melting away. *What if I'm not good enough?* she thought. "It's not too late for me to leave, is it?"

Batty raised an eyebrow. "Why do you want to leave?"

Autumn looked at her feet. "I'm worried I'm not going to be any good."

"You've always wanted to join a dance club."

Autumn knew Batty was right. Joining a dance academy had been her dream for ages and ages. She straightened up and pushed her shoulders back. I *can do this*, she thought.

Batty grinned at her, and Autumn was very glad her best friend was there.

Cosmic-Creeper sat inside one of the trophies on a low shelf, watching the witches.

"Warm-up time!" Verity called.

Everyone went through a series of warm-ups for about five minutes before Verity got the witches into lines. Verity was right – Autumn didn't feel as cold as when she first entered the gym. Batty fidgeted with excitement and checked her prosthetic leg, adjusting how she put her weight on it.

Verity clapped her hands for quiet. "Right then.

Is every witch ready to make a start?"

Suddenly, the gym door burst open and a witch with long green hair stalked in.

Autumn rolled her eyes. *Trust Severina to make a grand entrance,* she thought.

NUMBER ONE
DANCER!

VERITY PLACED her hands on her hips and raised an eyebrow. "Severina Bloodworth, I presume?"

Severina nodded. "Sorry, my dad forgot to give me a lift."

"OK, don't worry. Get warmed up quickly and join in," Verity instructed.

Severina hurried to the back of the gym, sticking

her tongue out at Autumn as she went past.

"We're going to look at some basic skills to begin with. I want to work out each of your strengths," Verity called.

Autumn closed her eyes and took a deep breath. *Nothing to worry about. Leif went through this with us already,* she thought.

"I'd like to see you all try a front walkover. Let me show you." Verity waved her arms in the air to create a magical demonstration. "*Sparkle, jump and prance, do a front walkover and dance!*"

A glittery figure appeared at the front of the gym and did a front walkover. Standing straight with arms raised skywards, the figure lunged forwards and raised one leg then the other and moved into a handstand.

Autumn's palms were cold and clammy, she trembled and imagined herself in a heap on the floor with everyone pointing and laughing.

"I'm going to use an anti-fall spell just to ensure that everyone feels confident and you can focus on getting those moves spot on," Verity said, as she swished a hand and a twinkling dust filled the air. The dust settled on the mats and Autumn thought the air smelt sweet.

Autumn's heart fluttered as she took a deep breath and launched herself into the move, leaving puffs of sparkly clouds behind her. She was relieved when she landed well and looked round to see how others were doing. She'd done it!

The coaches got everyone to try a whole range of skills: forward roll, backward roll and cartwheel. When Rainbow stood in front of Autumn and did a back walkover, Autumn's stomach felt like it had hit the bottom of a cauldron. This was one of the moves she struggled with. She nodded, took a deep breath and remembered all the practice she'd done with Batty.

Please, please let me be able to do it this time, Autumn thought and crossed her fingers for luck.

"OK, let's see you put the sparkle in Sparkledale Dance Academy!" Rainbow grinned, bouncing on the spot. "You can do it!"

Autumn positioned herself for a back walkover, stretching backwards and making herself look like a bridge. She brought her legs right over like she was walking in a circle through the air. Swirls of silver wrapped around her ankles as she moved. *I did it! A little wobbly, but I did it,* Autumn thought. Her cheeks ached as she grinned.

"Well done." Verity beamed at Autumn. "OK, I'd like to see some handstands into bridges." Verity looked around the room.

Verity chanted and the glittery figure showed the witches the moves to follow.

Autumn pushed and reversed into the move and landed well – creating a musical, shimmering bubble – but then she lost her balance and sprawled backwards. It was like she'd landed on an invisible marshmallow. The music stopped and the shimmering bubble popped. *At least the anti-fall spell cushioned me*, thought Autumn. Her cheeks felt warm and she slid off the magical cushion awkwardly.

Severina launched herself into a perfect move. The music she created gave Autumn a happy glow and shimmery bubbles floated above her. Severina flashed Autumn a smug grin as she stood up.

"Fantastic! I'm really impressed with everyone," Verity said.

Onyx gathered everyone into two different groups for tumbling.

"Yay, we're together," said Autumn, grinning at Batty.

"If you haven't done tumbling or you're not too confident with it, don't worry. Feel the positive dance magic vibes all around us." Onyx stretched her arms wide and closed her eyes for a moment as if she was concentrating. "We're going to do a jump sequence."

Autumn followed Onyx's instructions as they went through cartwheels and different tumbling skills. Her heart raced as she wobbled through some moves and made sludgy grey-and-brown swirls and out-of-tune music. Autumn was relieved a lot of the other witches around her were having the same problem, even Severina.

Rainbow demonstrated the sequence. Her movement was sharp and snappy as she jumped up with her legs horizontal. "Copy me!"

Autumn bit her lip before thrusting her arms towards the ceiling. She jumped with her legs raised up and toes pointed. Autumn was pleased, even if her legs weren't quite as high as they needed to be.

"Lift those chins." Verity walked past and a flying pen jotted down notes on a hovering clipboard.

Autumn's thighs and calf muscles ached as a warm furry body brushed against her.

"Hi, Cosmic-Creeper." Breathless, Autumn rubbed under his chin, making him purr happily.

"Good work, guys. Go and grab a drink," Verity instructed. She tilted her head towards Autumn. "Looks like Cosmic-Creeper has taken a shine to you. He only lets certain witches fuss him."

Autumn pushed her shoulders back, pleased at the compliment.

"This is amazing!" Batty grinned.

"Here you go, Autumn." Severina handed Autumn her water bottle.

That's weird, Autumn thought. *Why is she being nice to me?* Autumn and Batty exchanged puzzled looks, then shrugged and gulped down water.

Severina's water bottle had the words: NUMBER ONE DANCER across it. *Typical*, Autumn thought.

Verity stood in front of the witches with Onyx and Rainbow

either side of her. "Ready for the next section of today's training?"

Autumn took another big gulp of water, her throat dry with nerves.

A REAL
BLACK CAT!

AUTUMN STOOD and waited for the next instructions, wondering what might come next. Her tummy fluttered with excitement.

"We've choreographed a mini dance routine for you to copy," Verity beamed.

There was excited chattering around the room.

"Rainbow and Onyx will give a little demonstration."

Their moves created a harmony that sounded like flutes and fairy wings. Tiny silver butterflies fluttered above Rainbow and Onyx as they danced and moved around the gym.

"Magical!" Autumn breathed.

"I'll get you to go through the moves next, just listen to my count." Verity looked around the gym. "Everyone ready?"

Autumn was looking forward to trying out the moves. She wanted to be as good as Rainbow and Onyx.

"On the count of one, I want you to put your hand on your hip and your other arm in front – hold your hand like it's a scoop," Verity instructed. "I'll count slowly, just follow what Onyx and Rainbow do on each count."

Autumn followed each move, biting her lip as she concentrated.

"One . . . two, arm back to hip, other arm straight

in front . . . three, left and right arms stretched in the same direction."

"Pretend your arms are a broomstick sticking out to the side," Onyx said.

"Four, hands like an X across your chest one over the other . . . five, arms straight up, reach for the stars . . . six, hands on hips, tilt to your right . . . seven, switch and tilt to your left . . . and eight, switch and pose!"

Autumn could hear music beginning to play. The sound vibrated through the floor rippling up through her body.

"And one . . . two . . . three . . . four . . ." Verity counted them through each step.

Autumn felt like she was made of glitter as happiness sparkled from her.

Rainbow and Onyx danced at the front of the group, leading them through the count.

"Five ... six ... seven ... eight ... pose! Wooooh!" Verity cheered.

Autumn ended the routine by posing with her hands on her hips and feet about a shoulder distance apart. Her arms tingled . . . and it wasn't from the dance. They were stinging and itching like crazy. "Ouch!" Autumn said. "What's going on?"

Witches all around gasped as whiskers sprouted on Autumn's face, followed by a pair of furry ears and, finally, a long swishy black-cat tail.

Autumn jumped as Cosmic-Creeper emerged from a trophy, fur standing on end and hissing at Severina.

"Cosmic-Creeper?" Verity frowned. "Has Severina got anything to do with this?"

"I didn't do it," Severina squeaked. She backed away as Cosmic-Creeper let out another loud wail.

Verity looked sternly at Severina. "Cosmic-Creeper is exceptionally good at sniffing out magic.

If you hadn't been late to try outs you would have heard me mention this."

Severina looked at her feet. "It was just a joke. I used a potion to make her a proper *black cat* for a laugh."

Verity stood with her hands on her hips. "I'm afraid I'll have to talk to your parents about this."

Severina flapped her arms about.

"I will be telling them exactly what's gone on."

"No! You can't."

"It's against the rules to use magic against another witch in here. Not very team-like of you at all." Verity shook her head slowly.

"Don't tell my parents!" Severina pleaded, she had tears in her eyes.

"I just can't risk that sort of behaviour. Someone could get seriously injured."

"What? That's not fair! It was just a joke."

Autumn cleared her throat and tried not to miaow.

"We learnt this potion at school this week. Severina is in my class, so I know it was just a joke. Please don't tell her parents."

Severina smiled gratefully at Autumn.

"*Shiver and shine, a whiskery twitch, turn this cat back into a witch!*" Verity uttered a spell. A fluffy white cloud formed around Autumn and sparkled before it slowly turned furry and smelt of candy floss. The cloud flew up and away, out of a window, leaving Autumn tail-free and back to normal.

"There. Now let's have no more of this messing about," Verity said.

"Thanks, Moonbeam. I suppose you're not all bad." Severina nudged Autumn with her elbow playfully.

"Great training today, well done everybody. I'll be in touch by Monday with the results."

Autumn gulped and wondered if she'd done enough to secure a spot at Sparkledale.

A MAGICAL
MESSAGE

AUTUMN FOUND it hard to concentrate at school on Monday. She couldn't stop wondering if she had made it into the team.

She could barely eat her lunch, and it was her favourite. Autumn wished she could be as confident and chilled about it as Batty was.

Zephyr smiled reassuringly, guessing what Autumn must be thinking. "The odds are in your favour, you know. You're a really good dancer."

"Thanks," Autumn said, but her tummy was like a cauldron full of wriggling worms.

Leif kept telling bad jokes to cheer Autumn up, but nothing would shift the gloomy cloud of worry that was hanging over her.

"Who did the zombie take to the dance?" Leif asked.

Autumn shrugged in response. Even the word *dance* made her tummy cartwheel.

"His *ghoul*-friend. Get it?" Leif held his stomach he was giggling so much.

Autumn, Zephyr and Batty groaned.

"Seriously, Leif, you need some better jokes." Batty grinned at him.

"Want to play a game? It always relaxes me when I'm worried about something." Zephyr waggled a pack of cards.

"No, thanks. I just can't concentrate on anything."

Even Severina was quiet all day. She had a worried expression and chewed the end of her wand. *She was actually a pretty magical dancer,* Autumn thought – not that she'd ever tell her. But Autumn wondered if Severina turning her into a cat might have lost her chance at a place on the team ... then she'd probably blame Autumn!

Severina didn't tease Autumn once all day, even when she got her charms all wrong and accidentally turned Mr Snailcruncher into a frog!

Autumn hurried home after school. Her broom zipped and zoomed through the streets.

"Slow down!" Zephyr called from behind her.

"Any news yet?" Autumn asked, as soon as she burst through the front door at home.

"Not yet, pumpkin." Mum shook her head.

Autumn's brothers were arguing over the spell-a-vision handset in the living room whilst Trevor

flew over their heads, hiccupping tiny balls of fire and singeing the curtains. Weed was clapping and cheering him on.

"No, I'm choosing!" Mordecai shouted.

"No, I am!" Toadflax lunged for the handset, trying to push Mordecai off the settee.

"Neither of you will be watching anything if you don't stop that nonsense, RIGHT NOW!"

"Sorry, Mum," they said, dodging Trevor as he landed on the settee between them.

Autumn's heart skipped as a POP! followed by the tinkling sound of the message mirror filled the house. "Message for Madam Moonbeam."

"Hello?" Mum answered.

Batty's mum flickered into view and Mum chatted to her whilst Autumn hopped from foot to foot awaiting any dance-related news.

"Oh great, tell Edith well done from us," Mum said.

Autumn crossed her fingers and toes. *Please, please, please let me be in.*

"OK, thanks for letting me know. Bye!" Mum pressed a button and Batty's mum disappeared from the mirror.

"Well?" Autumn asked anxiously, her eyes nearly popping out.

"Edith is going to come round in a bit."

"Is that all?" Surely that wasn't the only thing Mum was talking about.

"Oh, and Edith has been offered a place at Sparkledale."

Autumn was really excited for Batty, but she was also cold and had goosebumps. *Surely I would have heard by now too,* she thought. She dodged Ghostly Gran who was floating by the kitchen table as Zephyr set out a chess board.

"I'm going in the garden!" Autumn called, trudging outside, her feet feeling about ten times heavier than usual.

Severina was in her garden too. Autumn wondered if she'd heard anything from Sparkledale Dance Academy. Severina came to the fence, eyebrows raised and looking expectant. "Well?" she asked.

Autumn shook her head. "Nothing. But I've just heard Batty got a place."

"That's it, then. I haven't got in." Severina slumped down and plucked at bits of grass.

If Severina hadn't got in, then Autumn was sure she wouldn't have either.

POP! A musical sound tinkled inside Severina's house. "Message for Severina Bloodworth from the Sparkledale Dance Academy!" a voice trilled. Severina raced into her house, leaving a thoroughly miserable Autumn behind. Autumn heard cheers and whoops from next door and guessed Severina had been successful after all.

Storm came strolling out from under the willow tree and nuzzled and purred against Autumn. She gave him a rub under the chin and stroked his velvety fur; giving him a fuss always made her feel a little better.

"Batty's here!" Mum called from the back door.

Autumn leapt to her feet as there was another loud POP! Followed by music coming from inside her house. She ran as fast as she could and burst into the kitchen to find Batty standing with her family and the magical mirror hovering in the air announcing: "Message for Autumn Moonbeam from the Sparkledale Dance Academy!"

This is it, Autumn thought and gulped, her throat suddenly very dry. *Will it be a no or a yes?*

Verity's face appeared in the mirror, with a beaming smile. "A good magical afternoon, Autumn!"

"Good magical afternoon!" Autumn said nervously.

Cosmic-Creeper appeared on Verity's shoulder and miaowed. "As you know, we had a lot of wonderful witches come and try out for Black Cats, and with only four spaces available at the moment I'm afraid it was a very difficult decision to make."

Oh no, here it comes, she's softening the bad news, thought Autumn.

"That's why I am absolutely thrilled to offer you a place with Sparkledale Dance Academy!"

Autumn couldn't believe it. She'd done it! "Thank you so much!" she said, beaming.

"I'll look forward to seeing you at training next week," Verity said, before waving goodbye and ending the call.

Autumn skipped and cartwheeled around the kitchen, leaving trails of rainbow sparkles all around.

Batty hugged Autumn. "We're both in Black Cats! How spell-tacular is that?"

"This is the best day ever!" Autumn said.

Autumn's family all cheered – even her brothers had come out of the living room to congratulate her. Trevor circled above their heads blowing little smoke rings. Ghostly Gran gave Autumn an icy high five.

"Told you you're a great dancer!" Zephyr said.

"Celebratory ice-screams, everyone?" Mum said, handing out cones filled with the noisy sweet treat.

"Yay!" everyone cheered.

"And how about an evening of your favourite dance show on the spell-a-vision?" Mum asked.

Autumn's older brothers groaned, Zephyr rolled her eyes but smiled, and Autumn and Batty cheered. "Dance! Dance!" Weed laughed.

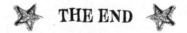 **THE END**

FIND OUT WHAT HAPPENS IN AUTUMN'S
NEXT ADVENTURE – COMING OCTOBER 2022

SPOOKY
SLEEPOVER

LEARN TO DANCE LIKE AUTUMN!

Follow the steps below to dance like Autumn in her audition for the Sparkledale Dance Academy!

Make sure you practise somewhere with plenty of space around you and where no one will bump into you. Dance warning – magic may happen!

ACKNOWLEDGEMENTS

So many people have helped me with Autumn and there's not enough room to mention everyone, otherwise I'd need a new book, *Autumn Moonbeam: The Acknowledgements*. Sorry if I've missed your name, but know I value and love you all!

I can't thank Hazel Holmes enough for welcoming Autumn and me to the UCLan family, Charlotte and the whole UCLan team and students, Becky Chilcott's amazing designs, Kathy Webb's fabulous edits and everyone else who has played a part in making my dreams come true.

Huge thanks to Heidi Cannon, whose beautiful illustrations have brought Autumn's world to life!

To the amazing Laura West, you took a chance on me and got Autumn out into the world. I can't thank you enough for all you have done in making my dream a reality and me a better writer.

Special thanks to Veronique Baxter, my lovely agent, and the amazing team at the David Higham agency.

Carolyn Ward and Tizzie Frankish, you need special medals for all your hand holding and generally being fabulous friends and excellent editors!

Amy Feest, Susan Mann, Melissa Welliver, Anne Boyere, Jeanna Skinner, Lorna Riley and Anna Orridge for always cheering me on, reading drafts and listening to my endless chatter of every stage of this journey. Dale Hannah and Debbie Roxburgh for brilliant beta reads and Tamsyn Murray and Stephanie King for casting your excellent editorial eyes over Autumn.

Thank you to my lovely writing friends on Twitter, the #ukteenchat gang, online writing groups, especially The Nearlies, my Debut 22 group, the SCBWI Central West crit group, Amie and

Charlie at Urban Writers' Retreat, and my local writing groups, Castlecroft Writers and Wombourne Writers, NAWG, Stuart White and everyone involved in the fabulous #WriteMentor community, so many lovely people!

Thank you to the Sharon Ann Academy of Cheer and Dance; when Poppy joined the club when she was three I had no idea how invested I would be in dance and cheer, and how it would spark the idea for Autumn Moonbeam.

Thank you, Mom, you gave me my love of reading and discovering the joy of visiting a myriad of worlds within books.

A HUGE thank you to my wonderful husband, Alex, who brings me cups of tea and pushes food at me when I'm lost in edits, and my amazing children: Keiran, Callum, Aidan, Poppy and Rowan, who are an inspiration.

HAVE YOU EVER WONDERED
HOW BOOKS ARE MADE?

UCLan Publishing is an award winning independent publisher specialising in Children's and Young Adult books. Based at The University of Central Lancashire, this Preston-based publisher teaches MA Publishing students how to become industry professionals, using the content and resources from its business; students are included at every stage of the publishing process and credited for the work that they contribute.

The business doesn't just help publishing students though. UCLan Publishing has supported the employability and real-life work skills for the University's Illustration, Acting, Translation, Animation, Photography, Film & TV students and many more. This is the beauty of books and stories; they fuel many other creative industries! The MA Publishing students are able to get involved from day one with the business and they acquire a behind the scenes experience of what it is like to work for a such a reputable independent.

The MA course was awarded a Times Higher Award (2018) for Innovation in the Arts and the business, UCLan Publishing, was awarded Best Newcomer at the Independent Publishing Guild (2019) for the ethos of teaching publishing using a commercial publishing house. As the business continues to grow, so too does the student experience upon entering this dynamic Masters course.

www.uclanpublishing.com
www.uclanpublishing.com/courses/
uclanpublishing@uclan.ac.uk